miffy the artist

dick bruna

One day Miffy went to a gallery.

She enjoyed looking at all the works of art.

She liked the different shapes she saw.

Miffy and Mother Bunny

looked at pictures together.

Some pictures make things look different.

Miffy had never seen a blue sun before.

Miffy likes apples.

She was very happy

when she found a painting of one.

It was bright red.

On the way home

Miffy kept thinking

of all the wonderful pieces of art

she had seen.

At home Miffy found some crayons.

They were green, yellow, red and blue.

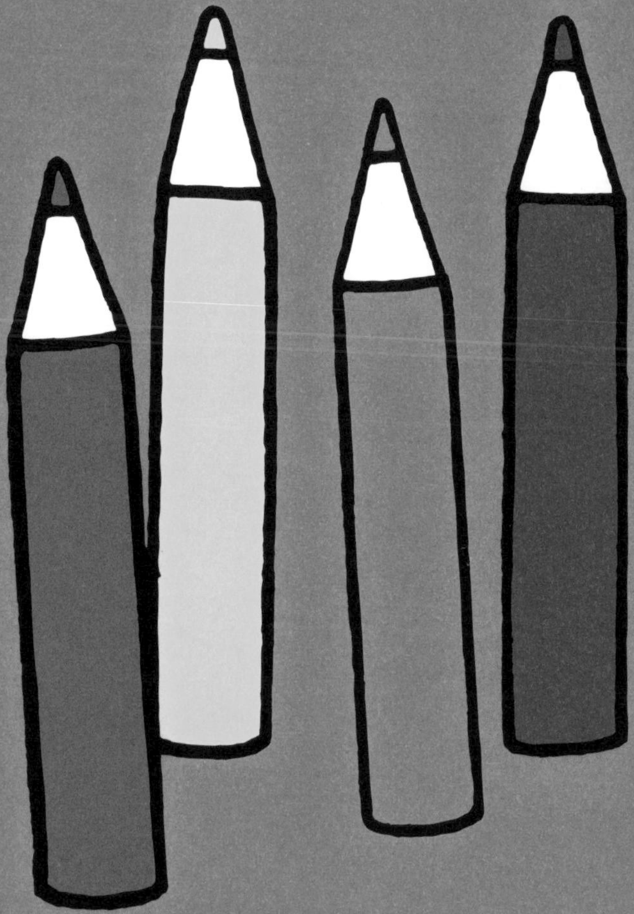

Then she found some paper

and made a picture.

First she drew some circles:

yellow for the sun,

green for a tree,

and blue – what a surprise! – for buttons.

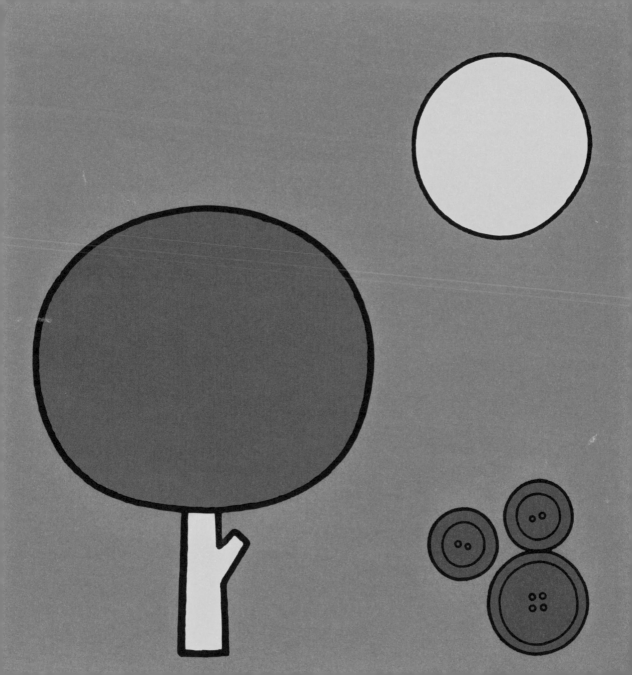

Then she drew squares and triangles.

They looked just like her

toy building blocks.

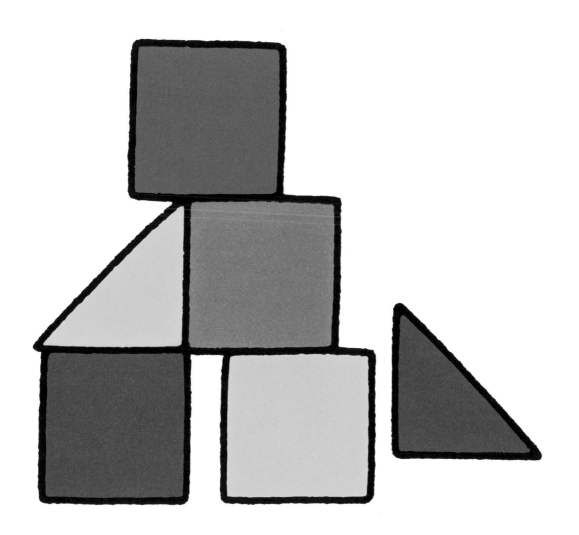

Next Miffy made a yellow picture.

It made her feel happy.

Then Miffy drew a picture in blue.

It made her think of a cold, cold day.

At the end of the day,

Miffy put all her pictures up on the wall.

'That looks wonderful, Miffy,'

said Mother Bunny.

'It's your very own gallery.'

Miffy tidied away her crayons and paper.

Tired but happy,

she knew she was a real artist.

When Miffy went to bed that night,

she did not need a bedtime story.

She was already thinking about all the

pictures she would make tomorrow.

Goodnight Miffy!